10/13

CALICO ILLUSTRATED CLASSICS

Kate Douglas Wiggin's

# Rebecca of Sunnybrook Farm

ADAPTED BY: Lisa Mullarkey

ILLUSTRATED BY: Eric Scott Fisher

magic
wagon

Published by Magic Wagon, a division of the ABDO Group,
8000 West 78th Street, Edina, Minnesota 55439. Copyright
© 2012 by Abdo Consulting Group, Inc. International copyrights
reserved in all countries. All rights reserved. No part of this
book may be reproduced in any form without written permission
from the publisher.

Calico Chapter Books™ is a trademark and logo of Magic Wagon.

Printed in the United States of America, Melrose Park, Illinois.
052011
092011
 This book contains at least 10% recycled materials.

Original text by Kate Douglas Wiggin
Adapted by Lisa Mullarkey
Illustrated by Eric Scott Fisher
Edited by Stephanie Hedlund and Rochelle Baltzer
Cover and interior design by Abbey Fitzgerald

**Library of Congress Cataloging-in-Publication Data**

Mullarkey, Lisa.
  Kate Douglas Wiggin's Rebecca of Sunnybrook Farm / adapted by
Lisa Mullarkey ; illustrated by Eric Scott Fisher.
     p. cm. -- (Calico illustrated classics)
  Summary: In early twentieth-century New England, talkative, ten-
year-old Rebecca goes to live with her spinster aunts, one harsh and
demanding, the other soft and sentimental, and spends seven difficult
but rewarding years growing up in their company.
  ISBN 978-1-61641-620-1
  [1. Aunts--Fiction. 2. Interpersonal relations--Fiction. 3. City and
town life--New England--Fiction. 4. New England--Social life and
customs--20th century--Fiction.] I. Fisher, Eric Scott, ill. II. Wiggin,
Kate Douglas Smith, 1856-1923. Rebecca of Sunnybrook Farm. III.
Title. IV. Title: Rebecca of Sunnybrook Farm.
  PZ7.M91148Kat 2011
  [Fic]--dc22                                              2011010667

# Table of Contents

# CHAPTER 1

# The Journey to Riverboro

The old stagecoach rumbled along the dusty road that ran from Maplewood to Riverboro. Although it was only the middle of May, it was as warm as summer. Mr. Jeremiah Cobb carried the mail in the coach along with one passenger. She was a small, dark-haired girl in a calico dress.

The child might have been ten or eleven years old perhaps, but whatever her age, she looked small. She was so slender and so stiffly starched that she slid from space to space on the leather cushions. Though she braced herself against the middle seat with her feet and hands, she bounced through the air as the coach bumped along.

When Mr. Cobb was about to leave the post office in Maplewood that morning, the girl's mother had said, "She needs to go to Riverboro." She helped her daughter, clutching a suitcase, into the stagecoach. "Take this bouquet of lilacs, too."

"Do you know Miranda and Jane Sawyer?" she asked Mr. Cobb. "They live in the brick house in Riverboro."

Miranda and Jane! He knew them well!

"They're expecting her. Will you keep an eye on her, please? Good-bye, Rebecca. Sit quiet so you'll look neat when you arrive. Don't be any trouble to Mr. Cobb."

"Good-bye, Mother," shouted Rebecca. "Don't worry. It isn't as if I hadn't traveled before."

The woman rolled her eyes.

"It was traveling, Mother," said the child eagerly. "I left the farm for a whole day."

The woman waved to her daughter. "Your aunts will be the making of you!"

Rebecca clapped her hands. Her journey to Riverboro had started! About a mile in, Mr. Cobb heard a small noise. He turned his head over his shoulder. He saw a small shape hanging as far out of the window as safety allowed. A long, black braid swung with the motion of the coach.

"Please let me speak!" Rebecca called. "Does it cost more to ride up there with you? The stage is too big for me. The windows are so small. I can only see pieces of things."

Mr. Cobb smiled. "You can come up if you want to. There ain't no extra charge." He helped boost her up to the front seat.

Rebecca sat down carefully. "Oh! This is better! I'm a real passenger now. I hope we have a long way to go!"

Mr. Cobb nodded. "It's about two hours."

"Only two hours?" she sighed. She looked forward to a long journey—one full of new sights and smells. She breathed in deeply. "It's a good growing day, isn't it?"

"Certainly is," said Mr. Cobb. "But it's a tad too hot. Why don't you put up your parasol?"

"Oh dear no! I never put it up when the sun shines. Pink fades terribly. I only carry it on cloudy Sundays. It's the thing I care most about, except my large family, of course."

"How many are there?" asked Mr. Cobb.

"Well, there's Mother and seven children. Hannah is the oldest. I come next. Then John, Jenny, Mark, Fanny, and Mira."

"Well, that is a big family!"

"Everybody says it's too big," said Rebecca. "Hannah and I haven't done anything but put babies to bed and wake them up in the morning. It's been that way for years and years. But we're finished with babies now. Mother says so. She always keeps her promises. There hasn't been any since Mira and she's three. She was born the day Father died on the farm."

"Oh, you live on a farm, do you? Where is it?" asked Mr. Cobb. "What's your folks' name?"

"Randall. My mother's name is Aurelia Randall."

"Your farm ain't the old Hobbs place, is it?"

"No, it's just Randall's Farm. At least that's what Mother calls it. I call it Sunnybrook Farm."

"I guess it doesn't make any difference what you call it as long as you know where it is," remarked Mr. Cobb.

Rebecca frowned. "Oh! Don't say that. Don't be like all the rest! It does make a difference what you call things. When I say Randall's Farm, do you see how it looks?"

"No, I can't say I do," said Mr. Cobb.

"Now when I say Sunnybrook Farm, what does it make you think of?"

"I suppose there's a brook somewhere near it," he said.

Rebecca looked disappointed. "That's pretty good," she said encouragingly. "There's a brook. It has young trees and baby bushes on each side of it. It has a white sandy bottom and lots of shiny pebbles. Whenever there's a bit of sunshine, the brook catches it. It's always full of sparkles."

"I know a lake like that in Milltown," said Mr. Cobb.

"Then I hope to see Milltown one day," said Rebecca. "I suppose it's bigger and grander than where I come from. Is it more like Paris?" She reached into her pocket. "My beaded purse is from Paris. Look how it opens with a snap. I've twenty cents in it. It's got to last three months for stamps, paper, and ink. Mother says Aunt Miranda won't want to buy things like that when she's feeding and clothing me."

Knowing Miranda like he did, he knew her mother was right.

"Paris ain't great," said Mr. Cobb. "It's the dullest place in the state of Maine."

"Oh, no, Mr. Cobb! Paris isn't in Maine. It's the capital of France," said Rebecca. "The French are such polite people."

He ignored her. "Milltown ain't great, neither. But if your Aunt Miranda will let you,

I'll take you down to Milltown this summer. As long as the stagecoach ain't full," he added.

"To think I should see Milltown! It's like having a fairy godmother who asks you your wish and then gives it to you! Did you ever read *Cinderella* or *The Fair One with Golden Locks*?"

"No," said Mr. Cobb cautiously. "Where'd you get a chance to read so much?"

"Oh, I've read lots of books," answered Rebecca. "I've read *The Lamplighter*, *Ivanhoe*, and *David Copperfield*. What have you read?"

"Nowadays I get along with the *Almanac*." He pointed to the green fields ahead. "When we get to the top of that hill, we'll see the chimneys of Riverboro in the distance."

Rebecca's hand stirred nervously in her lap. "I didn't think I was going to be afraid."

"Want to go back?" asked Mr. Cobb.

"I'd never go back. I might be frightened, but I'd be ashamed to run. Going to Aunt Miranda's is like going down the cellar in the dark. There might be ogres and giants under the stairs. But, as I tell Hannah, there could be elves and fairies and enchanted frogs!"

Mr. Cobb laughed at Rebecca. He admired her enthusiasm. "We've had a great trip. You won't forget about Milltown, will you?"

"Never!" she exclaimed. "And you're sure you won't, either?"

"Never! Cross my heart!" vowed Mr. Cobb.

"There's the stage turning into the Sawyer girls' place," said Mrs. Perkins to her husband. She saw a little girl in calico with flowers in one hand and a pink parasol in the other.

"That must be the niece from up Temperance way. It seems they wrote to Aurelia and invited Hannah, the oldest. But Aurelia said she could spare Rebecca better. She'll be good company for our Emma Jane."

There was no way for Mrs. Perkins to know that the girls would become kindred spirits.

It was a new day for Rebecca!

# The Spinster Aunts

They had been called the Sawyer Girls all their lives. Although Miranda and Jane were in their fifties, Riverboro still called them the Sawyer Girls. They were spinsters.

But Aurelia, the youngest, had married long ago. Her sisters called it a mighty poor decision. Miranda and Jane had washed their hands of Aurelia when she married Lorenzo de Medici Randall.

The sisters didn't trust Lorenzo's spending ways. He had a poetic way of using Aurelia's money to make investments for each child that blessed their union.

"A birthday present for our child, Aurelia," he would say. "A little nest-egg for the future."

Aurelia once remarked in a moment of bitterness that the hen never hatched anything out of them.

Having exhausted the resources of Riverboro, the couple had moved on. They settled in Temperance. That's where the money ran out.

The sisters wrote to Aurelia two or three times a year. They sent modest presents to the children at Christmas. However, they refused to assist with the expenses of the growing family.

It was several years since the aunts had seen the children. But they remembered that Hannah had not spoken a word during their time together.

"A perfect child," said Miranda. It was for this reason that they had asked for her to live with them.

Rebecca, on the other hand, had dressed up the dog in John's clothes. Then she was asked to get the three youngest children ready for dinner. She had held them under the pump to flatten their hair. They came to the table dripping mad. Miranda was disappointed in her behavior.

This memory of Rebecca was still fresh when they read Aurelia's letter. It stated that Rebecca, not Hannah, would be coming.

"I thought Aurelia would send us the one we asked for. It's just like her to hand off the rowdy one," said Miranda.

"We said that Rebecca might come in case Hannah couldn't," said Jane.

"I know we did. But we hadn't any notion it would turn out that way," grumbled Miranda.

"She was a small thing when we saw her three years ago," said Jane. "She's had time to improve."

"And time to grow worse!" said Miranda.

"Won't it be kind of a privilege to put her on the right track?" asked Jane timidly.

"More like a chore," said Miranda. "If her mother ain't got her on the right track by now, we sure won't.  I know Aurelia.  I've seen her house.  I've seen that batch of children wearing one another's clothes.  They never cared whether they had them on right side out or not. She'll have Hannah's shoes, John's undershirts, and Mark's socks most likely.

"I suppose she never had a thimble on her finger either.  She'll know the feeling soon enough.  I've bought a piece of unbleached muslin and brown gingham.  She can make a dress. That'll keep her busy."

"She may turn out better behaved than we think," said Jane.

Miranda gritted her teeth. Miranda Sawyer had a heart, of course. But she had never used it for any other purpose than pumping her blood.

Jane, on the other hand, had a tender heart. Maybe because Jane had known and lost love. She was engaged to marry young Tom Carter. Then the war broke out and Tom never made it home alive.

"You're soft, Jane," said Miranda. "You've always been soft and you always will be." She glanced nervously at the tall clock for the twentieth time. "The stagecoach ought to be here by now."

They both thought about Rebecca. But while Miranda wondered how they would endure Rebecca, Jane wondered how Rebecca would endure them.

The stagecoach finally rumbled to the side door of the brick house. Mr. Cobb helped Rebecca out of the coach. He introduced her to her aunts. She handed the bouquet of faded flowers to Aunt Miranda.

"You needn't have bothered to bring flowers. The garden's always full of them," Miranda replied.

Jane rushed forward to kiss Rebecca. "Put the trunk in the entry, Jeremiah. We'll get it carried upstairs this afternoon."

"Well, good-bye, Rebecca. Nice to see you both, Miranda and Jane. You've got a lively little girl there," Mr. Cobb said.

Miranda shuddered openly when Mr. Cobb said "lively."

"We're not much used to noise, Jane and me," Miranda remarked acidly. "I'll take you up and show you your room, Rebecca. Shut the mosquito netting door tight behind you. It will keep the flies out. It ain't fly time yet, but I want you to start right.

"Take your bag along with you. Rub your feet on that braided rug. Hang your hat and cape in the entry as you go past." She frowned when she looked at the parasol. "Lay your parasol in the entry closet."

"Do you mind if I keep it in my room, please?" asked Rebecca. "It seems safer."

"There ain't any thieves hereabouts. If so, they wouldn't want your sunshade. Come along. Remember to always go up the back way. We don't use the front stairs on account of the carpet. When you've washed your face and hands and brushed your hair, you can come down."

Miranda said nothing as she closed the door.

Rebecca stood perfectly still in the center of the floor. She looked about her. There was a square of oilcloth in front of each piece of furniture. A rug was set beside the bed. Suddenly, Rebecca felt overwhelmed. So much so that she tore off her hat and jumped under the bedcover.

Then the door opened quietly. "Rebecca!"

A dark, ruffled head and two frightened eyes appeared above the spread.

"Why are you laying in your bed? You're messing up the feathers. You're dirtying the sheets with your dusty boots!" screamed Miranda.

Rebecca rose. There seemed no excuse to make. "I'm sorry, Aunt Miranda. Something came over me. I don't know what."

"Well, if it comes over you again, we'll have to find out what it is. Smooth your bed this minute. Your trunk's coming upstairs. I wouldn't want our help to see such a mess. He'd spread it all over town."

Rebecca fought back tears. Her first ten minutes at the brick house told her all she needed to know.

She wanted to go home.

# CHAPTER
## 3
# Trouble at School

Rebecca had arrived on a Friday. On the following Monday, she began her studies. Miranda borrowed a neighbor's horse and wagon. She drove her to the schoolhouse down the road.

Rebecca walked the mile to school after that. She loved this part of the day best. When the dew wasn't too heavy, she took a shortcut through the woods. She turned off the main road. She waved away Mrs. Carter's cows, ran down a little hill, and jumped from stone to stone across a brook.

It was there that she'd climb a fence. Then she'd go through a grassy meadow, slide under another fence, and come out into the road again.

How delicious it all was!

Rebecca clasped her grammar and arithmetic books. She felt joyful knowing her lessons. Her dinner pail swung from her right hand. She always hoped to find a square of gingerbread inside. As she walked, she often recited a poem she was to present. All poems were expected to be memorized by Friday afternoons.

The little schoolhouse stood on the crest of a hill. Rolling fields and meadows were on the

left. A stretch of pine woods greeted students on the right. A river sparkled in the distance. Two doors led into the schoolhouse. One was for boys and the other for girls.

The teacher's desk and chair stood on a platform in one corner. There was a stove, a map of the United States, and two blackboards. A tin pail of water and dipper sat on a shelf. There were twenty wooden desks and benches.

Rebecca's teacher, Miss Dearborn, was puzzled by Rebecca. She didn't know which grade to place her in. So it was decided that she would read with Dick Carter and Living Perkins. She'd recite arithmetic and study geography with Emma Jane Perkins. History class would take place with Alice Robinson.

After a week, Rebecca stopped putting in extra effort in history. If she continued to progress, it would mean working with Seesaw Simpson.

He was called *Seesaw* because he couldn't make up his mind.

Seesaw stammered when he was nervous. He could never keep his eyes away from Rebecca. Her smile made him nervous. One day when Rebecca walked to the water pail, Seesaw did the same. But he couldn't get up the courage to speak to her.

The next day, Rebecca's thirst was great. When she asked a third time for permission to drink from the fountain, Miss Dearborn raised her eyes.

"What's the matter with you, Rebecca?" she asked.

"I had salt mackerel for breakfast."

For some reason, everyone laughed. Rebecca didn't mean to be funny. She spoke the truth.

Miss Dearborn did not enjoy jokes. She said, "You better stand by the pail for five minutes. It may help control your thirst."

Rebecca's heart ached. She couldn't move.

"Stand by the pail, Rebecca!" said Miss Dearborn. "Samuel, how many times have you asked for water today?"

"This is the f-f-fourth."

"I suppose you had something salty for breakfast?" asked Miss Dearborn with sarcasm.

"I had m-m-mackerel. J-just like Reb-b-becca."

Of course Seesaw was fibbing!

"I judged so," said Miss Dearborn. "Stand by the other side of the pail, Samuel."

Rebecca's head was bowed with shame. The punishment was bad enough. But to be punished with Seesaw Simpson was unbearable!

Miss Dearborn saw Rebecca's face. Tears hung on her lashes. Her breath came and went quickly. Her hands trembled.

"You may go to your seat, Rebecca," said Miss Dearborn a minute later. Then she leaned over and whispered. "I'm afraid I punished you more than I meant to."

"I hadn't missed a question the whole day!" said Rebecca. "I don't think I ought to be shamed for drinking. Sam Simpson is a copycat!"

"Maybe so," said Miss Dearborn. "Copycats often do things when they feel certain things in the heart."

Rebecca blushed. She vowed that she'd never speak to Seesaw Simpson again!

It was fortunate that Rebecca had her books and friends to keep her occupied. If not, life would have been dreadful in Riverboro. She tried to like her Aunt Miranda. The idea of loving her had been given up at the moment of meeting her.

Rebecca irritated her aunt with every breath she took. She continually forgot to use the back steps. She darted up the front stairs because it was the shortest route to her bedroom. She left the dipper on the kitchen shelf instead of hanging it up over the pail. She sat in the chair the cat liked best. But her biggest fault in her aunt's eyes was that she was a reminder of her foolish father.

*Now if Hannah had come*, thought Miranda, *things would have been fine in the brick house.*

Hannah took after the other side of the house. She was "all Sawyer." She spoke only when spoken to. She enjoyed knitting. Hannah would have been welcomed with open arms. But Miranda reminded Rebecca over and over again that she was a Randall. Just a Randall.

What sunshine in a shady place was Aunt Jane to Rebecca. Aunt Jane, with her quiet voice and understanding eyes, always had a kind word.

One day, Rebecca took her sewing and sat beside Aunt Jane in the kitchen. She finished her first brown gingham dress! Then she asked Aunt Miranda if she might have another color.

"I bought a whole piece of the brown," said Miranda. "That'll give you two more dresses."

"I know. But Mr. Watson says he'll take back part of it. We can have pink and blue for the same price."

"Did you ask him?"

Rebecca nodded.

"It was none of your business."

"I was helping Emma Jane choose aprons. I didn't think you'd mind which color I had. Pink keeps clean just as nice as brown."

"I don't approve of children being dressed in fancy colors. But I'll see what Aunt Jane thinks."

"I think it would be all right," said Jane. "No harm to let Rebecca have one pink and one blue gingham. It's only natural she should long for a change."

Aunt Miranda looked disappointed in Aunt Jane's decision. "I still don't know why you need to be in pink. You're lucky Aunt Jane agreed with you. I would have made you wear the practical brown forever."

Rebecca reached out and squeezed Aunt Jane's hand. As she started to sew her pink gingham, she said a prayer of thanks for Aunt Jane's loving ways.

# CHAPTER 4

# The Gingham Dress

Friday afternoon was always the time Miss Dearborn chose for reciting poems. Most of the children hated the burden of learning them. They dreaded the danger of forgetting them and being scolded.

But Rebecca had somehow brought a new spirit into these afternoons. She had taught Elijah and Elisha Simpson three funny poems. They left the teacher and students laughing long after they finished.

On this particular Friday morning, Miss Dearborn announced, "The exercises promise to be interesting, so I've invited the doctor's wife, the minister's wife, and two members of the school committee to come and enjoy them."

Living Perkins was asked to decorate one of the blackboards. Rebecca drew on the other. Living, the star artist of the school, chose the map of North America. Rebecca drew an American flag. She used red, white, and blue chalk.

Miss Dearborn was delighted. "Let's give Rebecca and Living a good clapping for such beautiful pictures. Pictures that the whole school may be proud of!"

The students clapped and cheered. Rebecca's heart jumped for joy. Dick Carter suggested that Living and Rebecca should sign their names to their pictures. "This way, visitors will know who drew them."

Miss Dearborn dismissed the morning session early. "Those who live near enough may go home and change."

Emma Jane and Rebecca ran every step of the way.

"Will your Aunt Miranda let you wear your best? Or must you wear your brown calico?" asked Emma Jane as they ran.

"I'll ask Aunt Jane," Rebecca replied. "Oh! If only my pink dress was finished! Aunt Jane was making buttonholes."

Rebecca found the side door locked. But she knew that an extra key was under the step. She unlocked the door and went into the dining room. Her lunch was on the table. Next to it was a note from Aunt Jane saying that they had gone to town.

Rebecca swallowed a piece of bread and butter. Then she flew up the front stairs to her bedroom. On the bed lay the pink gingham dress finished by Aunt Jane's kind hands! Should she dare wear it without asking?

*I'll wear it*, thought Rebecca. *They're not here to ask. It's only gingham after all.*

She unbraided her two pigtails. Next, she combed out the waves of her hair. After changing her shoes, she slipped on the pretty dress.

Then her eyes fell on her cherished pink sunshade! An exact match! She glanced in the parlor mirror. The dress was beautiful! It was made even prettier with the sparkle of her eyes and the glow of her cheeks.

Then she saw the clock. Goodness! It was twenty minutes to one and she would be late.

"Rebecca Randall!" exclaimed Emma Jane when she saw her at the schoolhouse. "You're handsome as a picture!"

Rebecca laughed and said, "Nonsense! It's only the pink gingham."

"How surprising that Miss Miranda let you put on your new dress!"

"They were both away and I didn't ask," Rebecca responded anxiously. "Why? Do you think they would have said no?"

"Miss Miranda always says no, doesn't she?" asked Emma Jane.

"Yes. But this afternoon is very special," said Rebecca. "Almost like a Sunday school concert."

The afternoon was indeed special. Perfect. Miss Dearborn received many compliments. She wondered whether they belonged to her or

to Rebecca. The child had no more to do than the others, but she stood out on stage with her remarkable enthusiasm.

Rebecca glided back home after school thinking about her day. It was a glorious feeling until she entered the side yard. That's when she saw her Aunt Miranda standing in the doorway.

"Step right in here, Rebecca. I want to talk to you. Why did you put on that good new dress without permission?" asked Aunt Miranda.

"I wanted to ask you at noontime but you weren't home," said Rebecca.

"You knew well enough that I wouldn't have allowed it," barked Miranda.

"If I'd been certain you wouldn't have let me, I'd never have done it," said Rebecca.

"And look at the other things you've done!" said Miranda. "You went up the front stairs to your room! I know because you dropped your handkerchief on the way up. You left the screen out of your bedroom window for the flies to come in. You never cleared away your lunch. And you left the side door unlocked for any thief to walk in!"

"Oh, I'm so sorry!" Rebecca cried. "I was late. It would be dreadful to get my first black mark on a Friday afternoon with visitors there to see!"

"I won't have you acting careless like your father. You're all Randall. Not a lick of Sawyer in you."

Rebecca's eyes welled up. "He was a perfectly lovely father. Don't speak badly about him."

"Don't you dare answer me back, Rebecca! Your father was a vain, foolish man. He spent your mother's money and left her with seven children to provide for," Aunt Miranda declared.

"It's something to leave seven nice children," sobbed Rebecca.

"Not when other folks have to help feed, clothe, and educate them," responded Miranda. "Now you step upstairs. Put on your nightgown. Go to bed and stay there until tomorrow morning."

Just then, Jane stepped into the room.

"Jane," said Miranda, "run outside and take the dish towels off the line. Shut the shed doors. We're going to have a terrible storm."

"We've had it just now," said Jane quietly. "I don't often speak my mind, Miranda. But you shouldn't have said what you did about Lorenzo. He was Rebecca's father."

Miranda growled. "That child will never amount to a hill of beans until she gets some of her father trounced out of her. And I'm just the one to do it."

Rebecca climbed the back stairs and closed the door of her bedroom. She took off the beloved pink gingham with trembling fingers. She braided her hair in pigtails and took off her best shoes. She plopped down on the bed and wished she could return to Sunnybrook Farm. Hannah should be sent instead.

Rebecca had thought Aunt Miranda might be pleased that she had succeeded so well at school. But there was no hope of pleasing her.

Rebecca clenched her fists and punched her pillow. Her mind was made up. She would slip away now. She was sure Mr. Cobb would keep her the night. She could leave for Sunnybrook Farm the next morning before breakfast!

Rebecca never stopped long enough to think about her plan. She put on her oldest dress, hat, and jacket. She wrapped her nightdress, comb, and toothbrush in a bundle and dropped it softly out of the window. She peered out the window and was relieved to see that the drop wasn't far below. Though had it been, nothing could have stopped her at that moment.

She scrambled out of the window and slid down the pipe. Then she jumped to the porch below. In a flash, she was flying up the road in a storm on her way to freedom.

# Tea with Mr. Cobb

Jeremiah Cobb sat at his table by the kitchen window. Looking up, the old man saw a figure of woe. Rebecca's face was so swollen with tears and misery that he almost didn't recognize her.

"Rebecca! My friend! Come in and dry yourself off." He took her hat and coat and hung them by the fire. "Why are you sad?"

"Oh Mr. Cobb, I've run away from the brick house. I want to go back to the farm. Will you take me up to Maplewood in the stagecoach?"

Mr. Cobb would do anything for Rebecca. "I suppose your mother will be glad to see you back again?"

A tiny fear in the bottom of Rebecca's heart stirred. "She won't like it that I ran away, I

suppose. She'll be sorry that I couldn't please Aunt Miranda. But I'll make her understand."

"I suppose she was thinking of your schooling by letting you come down here. But you can go to school in Temperance, can't you?"

"There's only two months of school in Temperance," sighed Rebecca. "The farm's too far from all the other schools."

"It'll be nice for all of you to be together again at the farm!" He waited to see her reaction. "You'll get to care for those little ones again. All day long, I bet."

Rebecca shifted in her chair. "It's too full. That's the trouble. But Jenny doesn't need as much looking after now." Rebecca bit her lip. "I'll make Hannah come to Riverboro."

"Suppose Miranda and Jane won't have her? They'll be mad at your going home, you know. You can't blame them," Mr. Cobb said.

This was quite a new thought to Rebecca!

"How is this school here in Riverboro?" asked Mr. Cobb.

"Oh, it's a splendid school!" said Rebecca. "And Miss Dearborn is a splendid teacher!"

"You like her, do you? Well, you'd better believe she returns the compliment. My wife saw Miss Dearborn on the bridge. You know what she said? She said 'Oh, Rebecca is the best student I have!'"

"Mr. Cobb, did she say that?" glowed Rebecca. "I've tried so hard! But I'll study the covers right off of the books now."

"You mean you would if you'd be staying here," said Mr. Cobb. "Now ain't it too bad you've got to give it all up on account of your Aunt Miranda? Well, I can hardly blame you. She's cranky and sour. Jane's a little bit easier, ain't she? Or is she just as hard to please?"

"Oh, Aunt Jane and I get along splendidly," exclaimed Rebecca. "She's as good and kind as can be. I like her better all the time. I think she kind of likes me, too. But she can't stand up for me against Aunt Miranda. She's as afraid of her as I am."

"Jane will be real sorry tomorrow to find you've gone away, I guess. But never mind. It can't be helped. She'll have to mend her broken heart," Mr. Cobb said.

There was a silence that could be felt in the little kitchen. Rebecca sat thinking. Finally, she pushed her teacup away.

"The rain has stopped," said the old man. "I'll be able to take you up the river tomorrow."

Rebecca rose from the table. She put on her hat and jacket quietly. "I'm not going to drive up river, Mr. Cobb. I don't know if Aunt Miranda will take me in after I've run away. But I'm going back now while I have the courage. Would you be so good as to go with me, Mr. Cobb?"

It warmed Mr. Cobb's heart that Rebecca had come to her senses. As he put on his jacket, he announced, "I have a plan. You can slip inside while I talk to your aunts about the wood I'm delivering this week. The front door won't be locked, will it?"

"Not this time of night," Rebecca answered. "Not until Aunt Miranda goes to bed."

The plan worked! As Mr. Cobb distracted Rebecca's aunts at the side door, Rebecca slipped in the front door. As she lay her head on her pillow, she felt a sense of peacefulness. She had been saved from foolishness. Her heart was softened now. She was now determined to someday win Aunt Miranda's approval.

Rebecca moved about the house the next day quiet as a mouse.

"I've never seen a child improve so quickly in her work as Rebecca has today," remarked

Miranda to Jane on Saturday evening. "That talking-to I gave her was just what she needed."

"I'm glad you're pleased," returned Jane. "A cringing worm is what you want, not a bright, smiling child. When she came downstairs this morning it seemed she'd grown old in the night."

Miranda brushed off Jane's remarks. But when she was alone that night, Miranda felt sorry for her hateful words. She thought of the Rebecca she saw that day working so hard. Maybe she had a little Sawyer in her after all.

To soothe Miranda's guilt, she finally allowed Mr. and Mrs. Cobb to take Rebecca to Milltown. Emily Jane joined Rebecca and they had a splendid day of sightseeing.

"That Rebecca is everything you said and more," said Mrs. Cobb. "I wouldn't be surprised if she's famous one day. She has a heart of gold and a sharp mind. It's just what Riverboro needs."

Mr. Cobb nodded. "I couldn't agree with you any more than I do now."

# Rebecca Meets Mr. Aladdin

One of the first families Rebecca met in Riverboro was the Simpson family. They were a large family very much like her own. And like Rebecca's, there was never enough food or money in the home. Rebecca felt a bond with them right away. Rebecca could see their house from the brick house. Although Aunt Miranda didn't approve, Rebecca and the Simpson girls became instant playmates.

Mr. Simpson wasn't around much. When he did come home, it was usually to look for handouts or money. Then he'd be off to see the world once again. The youngest Simpson girls, Clara Belle and Susan, were creative. They proved to have greater money sense than their father.

Although they weren't paid, they decided to sell soap to their neighbors from the Excelsior Soap Company. Their pay would actually be prizes that they picked out of a catalog. They had sold enough during the earlier autumn to get a child's handcart. It was perfect for rolling over the country roads.

They could have tried to win books or a chair. Surely the family needed both. But the young girls had their sights set on a lamp.

"Won't it look beautiful on the table?" asked Clara Belle.

They thought it would be fun to ask Rebecca to help. Rebecca in turn asked Emma Jane Perkins to help. "Won't it be fun to sell soap for the Simpson family? They do need all the help they can get!"

It was decided that this would be a grand adventure. On a Friday afternoon, the girls met in Emma Jane's attic to practice their sales speech. Rebecca's aunts were traveling to a funeral far away. Mrs. Perkins had agreed to watch Rebecca for the weekend.

Rebecca waved the catalog in the air. "We have to say exactly what's in the brochure," said Rebecca as she picked up a bar of soap. She pretended to knock on a door. Emma Jane pretended to open it.

"Can I sell you a little soap this afternoon?" asked Rebecca. "It's called the Snow-White and Rose-Red Soap. There are six cakes in an ornamental box. Only twenty cents for the white and twenty-five cents for the red. It's made from the purest ingredients. The Snow-White is probably the most remarkable laundry soap ever manufactured."

No matter how hard the girls tried, they would fall into a fit of giggles when each one gave the speech. After each had practiced it without cracking a smile, they knew they were ready. They rushed into the kitchen.

When they asked Mrs. Perkins if they could sell soap for the Simpson family, she hesitated.

If only Rebecca wasn't the niece of the difficult Miranda Sawyer. But when Mrs. Perkins thought about how the girls were so willing to help a family in need, she simply couldn't say no.

The girls took the horse and wagon and traveled to Mr. Watson's store. They asked that several large boxes of soap to be charged to Clara Belle Simpson's account. The boxes were lifted into the back of the wagon. Rebecca and Emma Jane were now ready for their adventure!

It was a glorious Indian summer day. It seemed impossible to think that Thanksgiving wasn't too far off.

It was clear from the beginning that people preferred to buy soap from Rebecca.

"You've sold three boxes," said Emma Jane. "I've only sold three bars. I'm glad it's your turn to knock on the next door."

The girls had decided that only one should go to the door at a time. If they went together, they may fall back into laughter.

Rebecca walked up the lane of a large brick house and went to the side door. Imagine her surprise when she saw a man sitting on the porch husking corn. He had an air of importance about him. He was clean shaven and good looking. Rebecca was a trifle shy of the stranger. But there was nothing to be done but explain her presence. So she asked, "Is the lady of the house at home?"

"I'm the lady of the house at present," said the stranger. "What can I do for you?"

"Have you ever heard of the . . . would you like, or I mean . . . do you need any soap?" asked Rebecca

"Do I look as if I did?" he asked.

Rebecca's face reddened. "I didn't mean that. I have some soap to sell. I mean, I would like to introduce to you a very remarkable soap. It's the best on the market. It is called the—"

"Oh! I know that soap," said the gentleman. "Made out of pure vegetable fats, isn't it?"

"The very purest," agreed Rebecca.

"I'm keeping house today, but I don't live here," explained the gentleman. "I'm just visiting my aunt. But she's in Portland today. I used to stay here as a boy. I'm quite fond of the spot."

"I don't think anything takes the place of the farm where one lived when one was a child," observed Rebecca.

The man put down his ear of corn and laughed. "You talk as if your childhood is a thing of the past!"

"I can still remember it," answered Rebecca gravely, "though it seems a long time ago."

"I remember mine well enough. It was unpleasant," said the stranger.

"So was mine," sighed Rebecca. "What was your worst trouble?"

"Lack of food and clothes."

"Oh!" exclaimed Rebecca. "Mine was no shoes, too many babies, and not enough books. But you're happy now, aren't you?"

"I'm doing well, thank you," said the man, with a smile. "Now tell me, how much soap should I buy today?"

"How much does your aunt have on hand?" asked Rebecca. "And how much will she need?"

"Oh, I don't know about that," said the man. "Soap keeps, doesn't it?"

"I'm not certain," said Rebecca. "I'll look in the catalog. It's sure to tell."

She took the document from her pocket.

"What are you going to do with the magnificent profits you get from this business?"

"We're not selling it to make money for ourselves," said Rebecca. "My friend, who is holding the horse at the gate, is the daughter of a rich blacksmith. She doesn't need any money. I'm poor, but I live with my aunts in a brick house. We're trying to get a lamp for some friends of ours. They are very poor and need some sunshine in their lives."

"I've known what it was like to do without a lamp," said the man. "How many more bars must you sell to get that lamp?"

"If they sell 200 more cakes, they can have the lamp by Christmas," Rebecca answered. "Then they can get a shade by summertime."

"I see. Well, I'll take 300 cakes then. That will give them a shade and all."

Rebecca had been seated on a stool near the edge of the porch. When she heard him ask for 300 cakes, she tipped over and disappeared into a lilac bush.

The man rushed to pull her out of the bush. "You should never seem surprised when you get a large order. You ought to have replied, 'Can't you make it 350?'"

Rebecca laughed. "I could never be so bold! What if your aunt doesn't like that kind of soap?"

"My aunt always likes what I like," he answered.

"Mine doesn't!" exclaimed Rebecca

"Then there's something wrong with your aunt."

"Or with me," said Rebecca.

"What's your name, young lady?"

"Rebecca Rowena Randall, sir."

"Do you want to hear my name?"

"I think I know already," answered Rebecca. "I'm sure you're Mr. Aladdin in the Arabian Nights. Oh, please, can I run down and tell Emma Jane? She must be so tired waiting." She didn't wait for his reply.

"Oh, Emma Jane! Emma Jane! We've sold out!"

Mr. Aladdin followed Rebecca. He smiled as he lifted the boxes out of the wagon.

"Can you both keep a secret?" he asked. "It would be a rather nice surprise to have the lamp arrive at the Simpson house on Thanksgiving Day. Wouldn't it?"

The girls nodded and thanked the stranger.

"Oh, don't mention it," said Mr. Aladdin, lifting his hat. "If you ever have anything else to sell, be sure to find me."

"I surely will, Mr. Aladdin! I surely will!" cried Rebecca, tossing back her dark braids and waving her hand.

"Oh, Rebecca!" said Emma Jane in a whisper. "He raised his hat to us and we're not yet thirteen! It'll be five years before we're ladies."

"Never mind," answered Rebecca. "We're the beginnings of ladies, even now."

"What was the nice man's name?" asked Emma Jane.

"I never thought to ask!" said Rebecca. "Aunt Miranda would say that was just like me. But I called him Mr. Aladdin because he gave us a lamp. You know the story of Aladdin and the wonderful lamp?"

"Oh, Rebecca! How could you call him a nickname the very first time you met him?"

"Aladdin isn't a nickname exactly. Anyway, he laughed and seemed to like it."

Thanksgiving couldn't come fast enough for Rebecca and Emma Jane. Exactly two weeks later, on Thanksgiving Day, the lamp arrived at the Simpson house. It was delivered in a large packing box. Seesaw took it out and set it up. Although there was no card, Seesaw knew of only one person who could arrange such a thing—Rebecca!

# CHAPTER
## 7

# A Thanksgiving Surprise

For the last twenty-five years, the Burnham sisters traveled to the Sawyer home for Thanksgiving. This year was no different. After dinner, Rebecca sat silently with a book after the dishes were washed. When it was nearly five, she asked if she might go visit with the Simpson sisters.

"What do you want to run after those Simpson children for on Thanksgiving Day?" asked Aunt Miranda.

"They have a new lamp. Emma Jane and I promised to go up and see it. We want it to be like a party."

"Where did they get the money to pay for it?"

"The children got it as a prize for selling soap," replied Rebecca. "I told you that Emma

Jane and I helped them the Saturday you were in Portland."

"It's the first time I ever heard the lamp mentioned," Miranda said. She handed Rebecca her jacket. "Well, you can go for an hour." Then she stared at Rebecca's dress. "What have you got in your pocket?"

"Nuts and raisins from dinner," said Rebecca. "I'd had enough. I thought if I saved these, it would make the party better."

Miranda started to protest but Aunt Jane stopped her. "They were your own, Rebecca. If you chose to save them to give away, it's all right. We ought never to let this day pass without giving our neighbors something to be thankful for."

Miranda was about to object when the Burnham sisters nodded approvingly. As Rebecca went out, they remarked that they had never seen a child grow and improve so fast in such a short a time.

"Of all the foolishness I ever heard of, that lamp beats everything. It's just like those Simpson children. I didn't think those children had brains enough to sell anything."

"One of them must have," said Miss Ellen Burnham. "The girl that was selling soap at the Ladd's house in North Riverboro was described by Adam Ladd as the most remarkable child."

"It must have been Clara Belle," said Miranda. "Has Adam been home again?"

"Yes, he's been staying a few days with his aunt. There's no limit to the money he's making. His aunt says he was so taken with the little girl that sold the soap that he declared he was going to bring her a Christmas present," continued Miss Ellen.

"Well, there's no accounting for taste," said Miranda. "Clara Belle's got red hair, cloudy eyes, and a crooked smile. But I'd be the last one to begrudge her a Christmas present. The more Adam Ladd gives to her the less the town will have to."

"Isn't there another Simpson girl?" asked Miss Lydia Burnham. "For this one couldn't have had cloudy eyes. Adam said it was her eyes that made him buy the 300 cakes. Mrs. Ladd has it stacked up in the shed."

Jane wondered, *What child in Riverboro could be described as remarkable? What child had wonderful eyes?* She knew the answer: Rebecca!

Meanwhile, the "remarkable" child had flown up the road and met Emma Jane on the path.

"Something awful has happened," cried Emma Jane.

"Don't tell me it's broken," said Rebecca.

"Oh no! It was packed in straw. Every piece came out all right. I was there and I never said a single thing about you selling the 300 cakes. We can do that together."

"*Our* selling the 300 cakes," corrected Rebecca.

"No, I didn't, Rebecca Randall. I just sat at the gate and held the horse."

"Yes, but whose horse was it that took us to North Riverboro? Besides, it just happened to be my turn. If you had gone in and found Mr. Aladdin, you would have sold the soap. But what's the trouble?"

"The family has no kerosene or wicks. Seesaw has gone to the doctor's to see if he can borrow a wick. Mother let me have a pint of oil but she won't give me any more. We never thought of the expense of keeping up the lamp, Rebecca."

"No, we didn't. But let's not worry about that until after the party. I brought a handful of nuts and raisins and some apples."

"I have peppermints and maple sugar," said Emma Jane. "They had a real Thanksgiving dinner. The doctor gave them sweet potatoes, cranberries, and turnips. Father sent meat. Mrs. Cobb gave a chicken and a jar of mincemeat."

At half past five, if one had looked in the Simpsons' windows, they would have seen a celebration going on. The lamp was placed in the far corner of the room on a table. The brass glistened like gold. The crimson paper shade glowed like a giant ruby. Everyone stood around the lamp and watched it glow. Finally, Rebecca dragged herself away from the enchanting scene.

"I'll turn the lamp out the minute I think you and Emma Jane are home," said Clara Belle. "I'm so glad you both live where you can see it shine from our windows."

Seesaw came in from the shed. "There's a great keg of kerosene out there. Mr. Tubbs brought it over from North Riverboro. He said somebody sent an order by mail for it."

Rebecca squeezed Emma Jane's arm. "It was Mr. Aladdin." They parted ways and ran down their paths.

Rebecca entered the dining room with a grin. The Burnham sisters had gone and the two aunts were knitting.

"It was a heavenly party," said Rebecca. "Come into the kitchen and look out of the sink window. You can see the lamp shining red just as if the Simpsons' house was on fire."

"It probably will be before long," observed Miranda. "I've got no patience with such foolishness."

Jane accompanied Rebecca into the kitchen. Although the glimmer she was able to see from that distance didn't seem dazzling, she tried to be as enthusiastic as possible.

"Rebecca, who was it that sold the 300 cakes of soap to Mr. Ladd?" asked Aunt Jane.

"Mr. Who?" asked Rebecca

"Mr. Ladd, in North Riverboro."

"Is that his real name?" asked Rebecca in astonishment. "I didn't make a bad guess after all. Emma Jane and I sold the soap to Mr. Ladd."

"Did you tease him or make him buy it?"

"Now, Aunt Jane, how could I make a grown-up man buy anything if he didn't want to?"

Aunt Jane still looked a little unconvinced. "I hope your Aunt Miranda won't mind. You know how particular she is, Rebecca."

Aunt Jane would go on wondering about the soap. Finally, she threw her hands in the air. *Yep, that niece of mine is remarkable. Plain and simple. She's a Sawyer through and through.*

# A Visit to Sunnybrook Farm

Rebecca spent the next several weeks preparing for Christmas. The house looked festive decorated with pines and ribbons. Rebecca worked hard to make presents for her family on Sunnybrook Farm. It was quite a difficult thing to do with only fifty cents in her pocket! Then she made a tea cozy with a letter *M* stitched on it for Miranda and a pretty pincushion marked with a *J* for Aunt Jane.

Christmas Day was a crisp, fresh, crystal morning. Icicles hung like dazzling pendants from the trees. The Simpsons' red barn stood out, a glowing mass of color in the white landscape.

Miranda, Jane, and Rebecca gathered by the tree in the early morning. Aunt Miranda had bought her niece a nice gray squirrel muff and scarf. Although Rebecca thought they were ugly and boring, she kissed her on the cheek.

But Aunt Jane had made her the loveliest dress of green cashmere. Rebecca begged to wear it that very day! Then there was a beautiful tatting collar from her mother to fancy up her dresses and some scarlet mittens from Mrs. Cobb. They would match the lovely handkerchief from Emma Jane!

After breakfast, there came a knock at the door. A boy asked if Miss Rebecca Randall lived there. On being told that she did, he handed her a box bearing her name.

"It's a present!" said Rebecca. "But I can't think who it could be from."

"A good way to find out would be to open it," remarked Aunt Miranda.

Once the box was opened, two smaller packages were found. Rebecca opened the one addressed to her. It was a black velvet case. When she lifted the cover, she saw a long chain

of delicate pink coral beads. At the bottom,
there was a cross made of coral rosebuds. A
card with "Merry Christmas from Mr. Aladdin"
lay under the cross.

"Of all things!" exclaimed the two old ladies,
rising in their seats. "Who sent it?"

"Mr. Ladd," said Rebecca under her breath.

"Adam Ladd! Well! Don't you remember
Ellen Burnham said he was going to send Rebecca
a Christmas present? But I never supposed he'd
do it," said Jane. "What's the other package?"

"It's for Emma Jane," said Rebecca. It was a silver chain with a blue enamel locket on it. Her name was engraved on the back. He had remembered them both! There was a letter that read:

*Dear Miss Rebecca Rowena,*

*My idea of a Christmas present is something entirely unnecessary and useless. I have always noticed when I give this sort of thing that people love it. So I hope I haven't chosen wrong for you and your friend. You must wear your chain this afternoon, for I am coming over in my new sleigh to take you both for a ride. My aunt is delighted with the soap.*

*Sincerely your friend,*
*Adam Ladd*

"Well, well!" cried Aunt Jane. "How kind of him! Now eat your breakfast, Rebecca. Then you can run over to Emma's and give her the chain."

Rebecca was too excited to eat, but eat she must. Aunt Miranda would never allow her to leave without doing so. Once she ate her last piece of bread and jam, she raced to Emma Jane's house.

Mr. Ladd arrived promptly at three o'clock. Five minutes later, they were off on a glorious sleigh ride. The three chatted away all afternoon. They felt like old friends. When Rebecca lay her head down on her pillow that night, she couldn't wait to see what the new year had planned for her!

It was a good thing Rebecca had such fond memories of Thanksgiving and Christmas. For the new year had many unpleasant things in store for Rebecca.

She soon found out that the Simpsons were moving. Not only did their moving sadden Rebecca, but she and Emma Jane's hearts grew heavy when they learned that Mr. Simpson had traded in the lovely lamp for a bicycle.

"At least they got to enjoy the light for a little bit," cried Rebecca.

Shortly after the family moved, Rebecca received shattering news from Sunnybrook Farm. Mira, the baby of the Randall family, had died. Mira had always been cared for by Rebecca, so she was particularly guilt ridden.

Aunt Miranda and Aunt Jane saw to it that Rebecca was rushed home. She was to spend two weeks with her grieving family.

It was a sorrowful homecoming for Rebecca. The death of Mira, the sadness of her mother, the isolation of the little house, and the lack of basics made for a gloomy farm.

Rebecca walked through all the old playgrounds and favorite haunts of her early childhood. The dear little sunny brook was sorry company this season. There was no water sparkling in the sunshine.

She sat by the brook near the end of her two-week stay and got lost in her thoughts. She thought about Hannah being stuck in this house day in and day out. There weren't many people in the area and it was lonely, especially when mother was too sad to talk. Rebecca started to put Hannah's needs above her own.

Hannah had never had a chance. She'd never been freed from the daily care and work of the farm. Yet Rebecca had enjoyed privileges thus far. Life at the brick house had not been a path of roses, but there had been comfort and the companionship of other children. There were many chances for study and reading.

Rebecca shed more than a tear before she knew what she had to do. "Hannah, after this term I'm going to stay at home and let you go away. Aunt Miranda has always wanted you. It's only fair you should have your turn."

Hannah was darning stockings. She threaded her needle and snipped off the yarn before she answered, "No thank you, Becky. Mother couldn't do without me. I hate going to school.

I can read and write as well as anybody now. That's enough for me. I'd die rather than teach school for a living.

"The winter will go fast, for Will Melville is going to lend me his mother's sewing machine. I'm going to make white petticoats out of the piece of muslin Aunt Jane sent. Then there's going to be a social circle in Temperance after New Year's. I'm not one to be lonesome, Becky," said Hannah, blushing. "I love this place."

Rebecca saw that she was speaking the truth. But she didn't understand the red cheeks until a year or two later.

# CHAPTER
## 9

# Life at Wareham

That fall, Rebecca did have a happy event occur. She entered Wareham Academy. It was decided that she would complete the four years of coursework in three years.

By the time she was seventeen, she had to be ready to earn her own living. She was expected to help provide an education for the younger children. It was an exciting time in Rebecca's young life. It was made even more so with the news that Emma Jane would be attending Wareham, too.

Rebecca and Emma Jane were to go to and from school on the train daily from September to Christmas. Once the cold winter months settled in, the girls would stay at Wareham. The weather would be too harsh for daily travel.

The town of Wareham was a pretty village with a broad main street. The street was shaded by great maples and elms. It had a blacksmith, a plumber, two churches, and many boarding houses.

Boys and girls came from all parts of the county and state to attend Wareham. Rich and poor were welcomed.

There was one particular teacher at Wareham that had a profound effect on Rebecca. Miss Emily Maxwell taught English literature and composition. She was not only a teacher, but she became Rebecca's friend.

One day, Miss Maxwell asked each new pupil to bring her a composition written prior to the year. This way, she'd know exactly what each student needed to learn. Rebecca lingered after the others left and approached the desk shyly.

"I haven't any compositions here, Miss Maxwell. I can find one when I go home on Friday. They are packed away in the attic."

"Did you choose your own subject?"

"No. Miss Dearborn thought we weren't old enough. I can write poetry easier and better."

"Poetry!" she exclaimed. "Did Miss Dearborn require you to do it?"

"Oh, no. I always wrote it. Shall I bring all I have?" She was thrilled when Miss Maxwell nodded.

A few days later, she saw the black book on Miss Maxwell's desk. She knew that the dreaded moment had come. She was about to find out exactly what Miss Maxwell thought of her talents! She wasn't surprised when she was asked to remain after class.

Miss Maxwell came and sat by Rebecca's side on the bench.

"Did you think these were good?" she asked, giving Rebecca the verses.

"Not very," confessed Rebecca. "But it's hard to tell by yourself. The Cobbs said they were wonderful. But when Mrs. Cobb told me she

thought they were better than Mr. Longfellow's, I was worried. I knew that couldn't be true."

Miss Maxwell felt Rebecca was strong enough to hear the truth. "Well, my child," she said, "your friends were wrong. You were right. Judged by the proper tests, they are pretty bad."

"Then I must give up all hope of ever being a writer," sighed Rebecca. She wondered if she could keep the tears back until she was dismissed.

"That's not true," interrupted Miss Maxwell. "Though they don't amount to much as poetry, they show a good deal of promise in other ways. You almost never make a mistake in rhyme or meter. Poetry needs knowledge, vision, experience, and imagination. You'll need to work on the first three. But I rather think you have a touch of the last."

Rebecca felt better. She was sure she would learn so much from Miss Maxwell!

"Now for the first composition," said Miss Maxwell. "I'm going to ask all the new students to write a letter giving a description of the town and a hint of school life."

"A letter from Rebecca to her sister Hannah at Sunnybrook Farm or to her Aunt Jane at the brick house would be dull. May I pretend I'm a different girl? Maybe an heiress? I shall be called Evelyn Abercrombie. My guardian's name shall be Mr. Adam Ladd."

Miss Maxwell looked shocked. "Do you know Mr. Ladd? He helps our school out by donating money."

"Yes, he's my very best friend," said Rebecca delightedly.

"Well then you shall see your best friend often, for he often stops by," said Miss Maxwell. "That is, when you're not working on your splendid idea."

Rebecca couldn't wait to share the news with Emma Jane!

The first winter at Wareham Academy was the happiest time of Rebecca's school life. She and Emma Jane were roommates. They had put their modest possessions together to make their room comfortable.

The room had a cheerful red carpet and a set of maple furniture. Mrs. Perkins had made curtains and bedding of unbleached muslin. She had trimmed and looped back the curtains with bands of red cotton. There were two table covers to match and each girl had her study corner.

When Mr. Aladdin's last Christmas presents were added, a Japanese screen for Emma Jane and the little shelf with books from English poets for Rebecca, they declared the room finished.

When the girls weren't taking classes, they'd cozy up in their room talking about their life back home or their current studies. On one such day, the door opened softly and somebody looked in.

"Miss Maxwell told me I should find Miss Rebecca Randall here," the man announced.

Rebecca sprang to her feet. "Mr. Aladdin! Oh! I knew you were in Wareham. I was afraid you wouldn't have time to see us."

Adam had not seen Rebecca for several months. They had much to talk about. Hours later, Adam got up from his chair.

"Well, little Miss Rebecca and Emma Jane, I must be going to Portland," he said. "There's a meeting of railway directors there tomorrow. I'm so glad your school was on my way. I accepted my position here in memory of my poor mother. Her last happy years were spent here."

"That was a long time ago!" said Rebecca. "May I see a picture of your mother?

Adam took out a leather case and gently opened it.

"Oh, what a sweet, sweet, flowery face!" Rebecca whispered softly.

"I was only a child and could do nothing to protect my mother. Now I have success and money and power. It's enough to have kept her alive and happy. My money seems so useless now since I cannot share it with her."

This was a new Mr. Aladdin. Rebecca's heart felt a throb of sympathy.

"I'm so glad I know," she said. "My mother is always sad and busy. But once when she looked at John I heard her say, 'He makes up for everything.' That's what your mother would have thought about you if she had lived."

"You are a comforting little person, Rebecca," said Adam.

As Rebecca rose with tears still trembling on her lashes, Adam looked at her suddenly with new vision.

"Good-bye!" he said, taking her slim hands in his. "How will Mr. Aladdin get on without his comforting little friend?"

"By coming back to see me often," said Rebecca.

He bowed and kissed her hand. "You can count on that, Rebecca Rowena Randall. You can surely count on that."

# CHAPTER 10

# More Challenging Times

The first happy year at Wareham Academy was over. Rebecca had studied during the summer vacation and passed her exams in the fall.

By the spring of the second year, she settled into a leadership role at Wareham. She was elected assistant editor of the *Wareham School Pilot*. She was the first girl to ever hold such a position!

During the long winter months, Aunt Miranda seemed crankier than ever. One Saturday, Rebecca ran upstairs and burst into tears.

"Aunt Jane, nothing I do suits Aunt Miranda," Rebecca sobbed. "She complains about everything I do or don't do. If I stay out of her way, she complains. If I go to her, she says I am in her way. She said it will take me my whole life to get the Randall out of me. I'm not convinced that I want it all out!"

Aunt Jane attempted to soothe her. "You must be patient," she said, wiping Rebecca's eyes. "I haven't been honest. Miranda isn't well. About a month ago, she fainted. Seems to me she's failing. She has other troubles too that you don't know anything about. Be kind to her. She needs kindness right about now."

All the ill feelings faded from Rebecca's thoughts. "Oh! The poor thing! I won't mind a bit what she says now. I shall serve her with a happy heart and a smile on my face. She's just asked me for some toast. I dreaded taking it to her. But this makes everything different. Don't worry, Aunt Jane. Perhaps her health isn't as bad as you think."

Rebecca served the toast and tea on their fanciest china. She placed a fringed napkin on

the tray along with a sprig of geranium. She wanted to make everything pretty for Aunt Miranda. *She must certainly need cheering up,* thought Rebecca.

"Now, Aunt Miranda," she said cheerily, "I expect you to smack your lips and say this is good. It's not Randall, but Sawyer toast."

"You've tried all kinds on me," Miranda answered. "This tastes good. But I wish you hadn't wasted that geranium."

Later that night, Rebecca tried to guess the mysterious troubles to which Aunt Jane had referred. She went over their conversation in her mind several times. She simply couldn't figure out what bothered her aunt so. There was no way for Rebecca to know that all of her aunts' investments were lost. They were bankrupt.

"Can we possibly go on paying her school bills? Shouldn't we tell her? She'll understand," said Jane tearfully to her sister. "She'd want to know and do the right thing."

"Nonsense," said Miranda. "We've taken

her away from her mother. We offered her an education. We've got to keep our word. If we don't keep it, what good is our word? She's Aurelia's only hope now that Hannah thinks of nothing but that boy. We'll skimp and do without so Rebecca doesn't have to. I don't want her to know a thing. Do you understand, Jane? Not one little detail."

Rebecca, who knew nothing of their business affairs, didn't notice any change around the house. She saw her aunts pinch here and there, but she was used to that from living at Sunnybrook Farm for so long. If she hadn't had so much to worry about, maybe she would have noticed less meat and fish were bought or that the woman who helped wash and iron was dismissed.

There was, however, no concealing the state of things at Sunnybrook. The potato crop had failed. There were no apples to speak of. The hay had been poor. Aurelia had bouts of dizziness in her head and Mark broke his ankle. The time for paying the interest on the mortgage had come and gone. There was no possibility of paying the required forty-eight dollars. It was the first time in fourteen years that Aurelia couldn't keep a payment.

The only bright spot on the horizon was Hannah's engagement to Will Melville. He was a young farmer whose land joined Sunnybrook. He had a good house but was alone in the world. Hannah was so blinded by love that she hardly realized her mother's problems.

One day, Hannah surprised Rebecca and journeyed to the brick house. But she was a changed girl. She spoke endlessly of Will. She turned her nose up at any talk of the children.

Miranda's feelings about Hannah changed. "She's a selfish one. She told me she's not going to burden Will with her mother's ills. She's a Randall through and through! I'm glad to see her leave for Temperance. If that mortgage is ever cleared from the farm, it won't be Hannah that'll do it. It'll be Rebecca or me!"

# CHAPTER
## 11
# Mr. Ladd's Plans

Adam Ladd sometimes went to Temperance on business. He was involved in the proposed branch of the railroad. While there, he heard all the Sunnybrook news. He knew that Rebecca's family had fallen on hard times.

The building of the new road was not yet certain. There was a difference of opinion as to the best route from Temperance to Plumville. One way would lead directly through Sunnybrook. Mrs. Randall would be compensated. Her land would not be affected at all the other way. She'd receive no money. Adam decided to do his best to get the railroad to cross their property. He knew it would make all the difference in the Randalls' lives.

Coming from Temperance to Wareham one day, Adam took a long walk with Rebecca. He thought she looked pale and thin.

Adam looked at her in a way that made her put her hands over her face. She laughed through them shyly and said, "I know what you are thinking, Mr. Aladdin. My dress is an inch longer than last year and my hair different. But I'm not nearly a young lady yet. Sixteen is a month off.

"When you bought the soap, I thought you were grandfather Sawyer's age. When you danced with me at the flag-raising, you seemed like my father. But when you showed me your mother's picture, I felt as if you were my brother, John."

"I'm thinking nothing but how lovely you look. Lovely but tired. Are you studying too much?" Adam asked.

"Just a little," she confessed, "but vacation comes soon."

"Are you going to have a good rest and try to recover your dimples? They are really worth preserving."

A shadow crept over Rebecca's face. "Don't be kind, Mr. Aladdin. I can't bear it. It's not one of my dimply days!" Then she ran in at the seminary gate and disappeared with a wave of her hand.

Adam found his way to the principal's office. He had come to Wareham to hatch a plan that he'd been considering for days. This year was the fiftieth anniversary of the founding of the Wareham School. He intended to celebrate it by offering prizes in English composition. It was a subject in which he was much interested.

He wanted the boys and girls of the two upper classes to compete. The award would be made to the writers of the two best essays. As to the nature of the prizes, he had not quite made up his mind. He only knew they would be substantial ones. Perhaps books. Maybe money.

While waiting for the principal, he saw Miss Maxwell. He had scarcely greeted her when he said, "Miss Maxwell, doesn't it strike you that Rebecca looks tired?"

"She does indeed. I'm considering whether I can take her away with me. I always go south for the spring vacation. I travel by sea to Old Point Comfort. I should like nothing better than to have Rebecca for a companion."

"Why not let me help?" said Adam. "I'm greatly interested in the child. I have been for years." He told Miss Maxwell the circumstances of his first meeting with Rebecca. "From the beginning, I've tried to think of a way I could be helpful in her development.

"I interviewed her aunts years ago," he continued. "I had hoped I might be permitted to give her a musical education. I assured them I had her best interests in mind. I was willing to be repaid later on if they insisted. But it was no use. The elder Miss Sawyer remarked that no member of her family ever had lived on charity. Then she said she guessed they wouldn't begin at this late day."

"Rebecca does fine for herself, Mr. Ladd. With your help and heaven above, she'll be just fine."

Mr. Ladd sighed. "I hope so, Miss Maxwell. I pray so."

# CHAPTER
## 12

# Graduation at Last

A year had passed and graduation was about to be celebrated.

Rebecca got out of bed and crept to the window. She threw open the blinds and welcomed the rosy light. Even the sun looked different somehow. It was larger, redder, more important than usual.

Mothers and fathers of the students, as well as relatives, had been arriving on the train since breakfast time.

Old pupils, both married and single, with and without families, streamed back to the dear old village.

Before the ceremony started, Emma Jane and Rebecca sat in their room. Emma Jane wiped a tear away. She knew it was the last day that they would be together. The beginning of the end of their carefree days seemed to have dawned.

Two positions had been offered to Rebecca. One was near Augusta, but the other was more prestigious. It was as an assistant in the Edgewood schools. Although neither paid well, Miss Maxwell thought the assistant job would be more valuable.

"Emmie, don't you dare cry," Rebecca told her friend. "I'm on the brink myself! If only you were graduating with me. That's my only sorrow. There! I hear the rumble of the wheels. People are ready to see our grand surprise now. Hug me once for luck, dear Emmie."

Ten minutes later, Adam Ladd, who had just arrived from Portland, came into the main street. He stopped under a tree expecting the graduates to march by at any moment. What a surprise Wareham had in store for the crowd. Minutes later, Rebecca and her classmates drove through the streets on a decorated wagon. And who was driving the wagon? The student who

finished first in the class: Rebecca! She made a show of it and waved to the crowds as she passed.

Rebecca saw Hannah and her husband in the audience. She spotted the Cobbs, too. She felt a pang at the absence of her mother. Poor Aurelia had to stay behind at Sunnybrook. She had to care for the children. That, and a lack of money and a suitable dress, made the trip impossible.

There were other Riverboro faces in the crowd. Aunt Jane wasn't one of them. Aunt Miranda had not intended to come. Rebecca didn't expect her. She knew she wasn't up for the celebration. But where, on this day of days, was her beloved Aunt Jane?

However, this thought, like all others, came and went in a flash. For the whole morning was like a series of magic lantern pictures. They crossed and recrossed her field of vision. At the ceremony, she sang and recited Queen Mary's Latin Prayer.

Then the principal announced the winners of the writing contest. There were two names to be read. One award went to a young man and the other went to Rebecca! She could barely believe her ears when she heard the news. She was only brought back to the real world when she met Mr. Aladdin's eyes.

Then it was announced that they had won gold coins! She could finally pay off her mother's mortgage on Sunnybrook Farm!

At the end of the program came her class poem, "Makers of Tomorrow." And there, as on many a former occasion, her personality showed through. Her voice, her eyes, and her body breathed conviction, earnestness, and emotion. When she left the platform, the audience felt that they had listened to a masterpiece.

Finally, it was over. The diplomas were presented. Rounds of applause greeted each graduate at this thrilling moment. Jeremiah Cobb clapped louder than anyone. He was the talk of Wareham and Riverboro for days.

Yes, it was over. Afterward, the crowd thinned a little. Adam Ladd made his way to the platform. Rebecca turned from speaking to some strangers and met him in the aisle.

"Oh, Mr. Aladdin, I'm so glad you could come! Tell me, Mr. Aladdin, were you satisfied?"

"More than satisfied!" he said. "Glad I met the child, proud I know the girl, longing to meet the woman!"

Rebecca's heart fluttered at this sweet praise from her hero's lips. But before she found words to thank him, Mr. and Mrs. Cobb approached her. She introduced them to Mr. Ladd.

"Where is Aunt Jane?" she asked.

"I'm sorry, lovey. We've got bad news for you," said Mr. Cobb.

"Is Aunt Miranda worse? She is! I can see it by your looks!" said Rebecca as all color faded from her cheeks.

"She had a second stroke yesterday morning," said Mrs. Cobb. "Jane said you weren't to know anything until the graduation was over. We promised to keep it a secret until then."

Rebecca started to weep. "I'll go right home with you now. Poor Aunt Miranda! And I've been so happy all day except that I was longing for Mother and Aunt Jane."

"There ain't no harm in being happy," said Mr. Cobb. "That's what Jane wanted you to be. And Miranda's got her speech back. That's good news."

Emma Jane had just joined the group. She overheard the terrible news.

"I'll pack your trunk for you, Becky," she promised.

"Do you think Miss Sawyer's condition is serious?" asked Adam.

"Well, the doctor doesn't seem to know," said Mrs. Cobb. "Anyhow, she's paralyzed and she'll never walk again. Poor soul! She ain't lost her speech though. That'll be a comfort to her."

Adam left the church. When he crossed the common, he came upon Miss Maxwell. Knowing that she was deeply interested in Rebecca's plans, he told her the news.

"Rebecca must leave Wareham for Riverboro tonight. Her aunt is ill," he announced.

Miss Maxwell sat down on a bench. "That's almost more than I can bear! It seems to me that Rebecca never has a break. I had so many plans for her. Now she'll have to settle down to housework again. She'll be responsible for nursing that poor, sick, cranky aunt."

"If it had not been for the cranky old aunt, Rebecca would still be at Sunnybrook," said Adam. "She would have had no real educational training. I believe, though, that happier days are dawning for her," continued Adam. "It must be a secret for the present, but Mrs. Randall's farm will be bought by the new railroad. We must have right of way through the land. The station will be built on her property. She will receive 6,000 dollars. Although not a fortune, she'll get 300 or 400 dollars a year."

Miss Maxwell sighed, "I confess I wanted Rebecca to have a career."

"I don't," said Adam promptly.

"Of course you don't. Men have no interest in the careers of women! But I know Rebecca better than you."

"You may understand her mind better, Miss Maxwell, but not her heart. For no one understands her heart more than the man who met her selling soap so many years ago."

# News from Hannah

Rebecca didn't see her Aunt Miranda until she had been at the brick house for several days. Miranda refused to have anyone but Jane in the room. But her door was always ajar. Jane thought she liked to hear Rebecca's quick step.

Her mind was perfectly clear now. Although she couldn't move, she was free from pain. She knew everything that went on within the house.

"Were the windfall apples being picked up for sauce?" she asked. "Were the potatoes thick in the hills? Was the corn crop a good one?"

There came a morning when she asked for Rebecca. The door was opened into the dim sickroom. Rebecca stood there with the sunlight behind her. Her hands were full of sweet peas.

Miranda's pale, sharp face, framed in its nightcap, looked haggard on the pillow.

"Come in," she said. "I ain't dead yet. Don't mess up the bed with them flowers!"

"Oh, no! They're going in a glass pitcher," said Rebecca. She turned to the washstand as she tried to control her tears.

"Let me look at you. I hope you're not messing up the kitchen. I'm not there to clean it up."

"No messes, Aunt Miranda. Promise."

There was a long pause during which Rebecca sat down by the bedside and timidly touched her aunt's hand. Her heart swelled with pity.

"You're not to be anxious about anything," Rebecca said. "I'm all grown up and graduated. Good positions have been offered to me already. If you want me near, I'll take the Edgewood position. That way, I can be here nights and Sundays to help. If you get better, then I'll go to Augusta, for that pays a hundred dollars more."

"You listen to me," said Miranda. "Take the best place, regardless of my sickness. I'd like to live long enough to know you've paid off that mortgage."

The days went on. Miranda grew stronger and stronger. Before long she could be moved into a chair by the window.

Little by little, hope stole back into Rebecca's young heart. Aunt Jane began to press her handkerchiefs and collars. "I want you ready at any moment to go to Brunswick when the doctor says Miranda is out of danger."

They were sure it would be any day now!

Everything beautiful was to happen in Brunswick if she could be there by August. For she was to be Miss Emily's very own visitor and sit at the table with college professors!

The day dawned when the few simple dresses were packed in the trunk. Also added were her beloved coral necklace, her graduation dress, and her class pin.

Then, when all was ready, a telegram arrived from Hannah. "Come at once. Mother has had a bad accident."

In less than an hour, Rebecca was on her way to Sunnybrook. Her heart beat with fear as to what might be awaiting her at the farm.

It was not death. Thank the heavens for that!

Her mother had been standing on the hayloft and she slipped. Her right knee was broken and her back was strained. But she was awake and in no immediate danger.

When Aunt Jane and Aunt Miranda got news of Aurelia's health, Miranda grumbled. "Now she'll probably be a cripple. Rebecca will have to nurse her instead of earning a good income somewhere else."

"Her first duty is to her mother," said Aunt Jane. "I hope she'll always remember that."

"Nobody remembers anything they'd ought to at seventeen," responded Miranda. "Now that I'm strong again, there are things I want to settle. When I'm gone, do you want to take

Aurelia and the children down here to the brick house? There's an awful lot of them."

Jane smiled. "I'll do whatever you feel is best."

"Don't tell Rebecca but I've willed her the brick house. She won't get it until I'm gone. I want to take my time dying, you know. And I don't want to be thanked, neither. I suppose she'll use the front stairs, but maybe since I'm dead I won't mind."

There was a long pause. Jane sat and knitted silently as she wiped the tears from her eyes. "You're a good woman, Miranda Sawyer. A good woman, indeed."

Two months had gone by. They were two months of cooking, washing, and caring for the three children at Sunnybrook Farm. They were months in which there had been many a weary night of watching over Aurelia's bedside.

Aurelia was growing stronger. She could now smile at the past agony and forget the weary hours. But Aurelia worried about Rebecca. She knew that no girl of seventeen could pass through

such an ordeal and come out unchanged. She was doing tasks in which she could not be fully happy.

Aurelia and Hannah had fallen into a familiar pattern the last few years. Life was dull around the farm. But then Rebecca returned. Rebecca brought color and grace and harmony into the gloomy home. Rebecca gave her hope.

On a glorious morning, Aurelia asked to be brought to the window. The air was fragrant with ripening fruit. There was a mad little bird on a tree singing with the joy of living. He had forgotten that summer was over and that winter must come. But who could think of cold winds or frozen streams on such a day?

Then suddenly, Aurelia covered her eyes and cried, "I can't bear it! Here I lie chained to this bed and interfering with everything you want to do. It's all wasted! All my saving and doing without. All your studying. Everything that we thought was going to be the making of you! Gone."

"Mother, don't talk like that," said Rebecca.

"You can put a brave face on it," sobbed Aurelia, "but you can't deceive me. You've lost your place. You'll never see your friends here. You're nothing but a caregiver of the sick!"

"I may look like a drudge," said Rebecca with laughing eyes, "but I'm really a princess."

Aurelia smiled in spite of herself and was comforted. "I only hope you won't have to wait too long for your throne, Rebecca. But life looks very hard and rough to me. With your Aunt Miranda a cripple and me another here at the farm, you're tied hand and foot. Not just with me but with Jenny, Fanny, and Mark!"

"Why, Mother!" cried Rebecca, clasping her knees with her hands. "When you were seventeen, wasn't it good just to be alive?"

"No," said Aurelia. "But I wasn't so much alive as you are."

"Look," said Rebecca. She pointed to a coach coming up the drive. "It's Will! He ought to have a letter from the brick house."

# A New Beginning

Will drove up to the farm and gave Rebecca a letter.

"Miranda mustn't be worse," sighed Aurelia, "or Jane would have telegraphed. See what she says."

Rebecca opened the envelope and read the note aloud:

*Your Aunt Miranda passed away an hour ago. Come at once if your mother can spare you. I won't have the funeral until you're here. She died very suddenly and without any pain. Oh, Rebecca! I long for you so!*

*Aunt Jane*

Rebecca burst into tears. "Poor, poor Aunt Miranda! I couldn't say good-bye to her! Poor, lonely Aunt Jane! What can I do, Mother? I feel torn in two between you and the brick house."

"You must go this very instant," said Aurelia. "Your aunts have done everything in the world for you. It's your turn to pay back some kindness. The doctor says I've turned the corner. Jenny can help. Maybe Hannah will stop by."

It was decided. Rebecca must return to the brick house at once. She flew down the hill to get a last pail of spring water. As she lifted the bucket from the water, she saw a company of surveyors. They were busy with their instruments making calculations and laying lines for the railroad. She caught her breath. It was to happen after all!

*The time has come!* she thought. *I'm saying good-bye to Sunnybrook Farm forever.*

Will drove Rebecca back to the station. When he heard about the railroad, he said, "Cheer up, Becky! You'll find your mother sitting up when you come back. The next thing you know, the whole family will be moving to some nice little house wherever your work is. Things will never be as bad as they have been this last year. That's what Hannah and I think." He dropped her off at the depot and waved as he drove away to tell his wife the news.

Rebecca was overjoyed to see Mr. Cobb holding the horses' reins when she arrived in Riverboro.

"Oh, Mr. Cobb!" she sobbed. "So much has happened! We've had so many talks about Aunt Miranda and now she's gone. Gone!"

They drove on in silence but it was a sweet, comforting silence to both of them. Rebecca felt calmed by the familiar rolling meadows, the stately elms, the glowing maples, and the hollyhocks. The brick house came next. It looked just as she left it. Rebecca somehow thought it would look different without Aunt Miranda living and breathing inside.

"Stop, Mr. Cobb. I want to run up the path by myself." She jumped onto the path.

The house door opened just as Rebecca closed the gate behind her. Aunt Jane came down the stone steps. She looked frail. Rebecca held out her arms and the old woman crept into them.

"Rebecca," she said, raising her head, "do you feel any bitterness over anything she ever said to you?"

Rebecca's eyes glistened. "Oh, Aunt Jane! I feel nothing but gratitude for all she's done for me."

"She was a good woman, Rebecca. She had a quick temper and a sharp tongue, but she wanted to do right. She did the best she could. She never said so, but I'm sure she was sorry for every harsh word she spoke to you. Now let me tell you something, Rebecca. Your Aunt Miranda has willed all this to you!"

She flung her hands into the air. "The brick house, the buildings, the furniture. Even the land as far as you can see, is yours."

Rebecca threw off her hat and put her hand to her heart. After a moment's silence she asked to be left alone.  Rebecca sat in the quiet doorway, shaded from Riverboro by the overhanging elms.

A feeling of thankfulness and peace came over her.  She put up her hand and touched the shining brass knocker.  She ran her hands along the red bricks, which glowed in the October sun.

It was home.  It was a new life.  Her mother would once again have her sister and friends. The children would have teachers and playmates— more than they could count!

And Rebecca?  She wondered what life had in store for her. Would she be a writer? A teacher? Her heart skipped a beat when she thought of the endless possibilities.

She wondered about Mr. Ladd and how he would fit into her future.  She was certain he would and looked forward to their next meeting.

She closed her eyes and whispered, "God bless Aunt Miranda.  God bless the brick house that was.  God bless the brick house that is to be!"